Terry Jones

The Beast with a Thousand Teeth

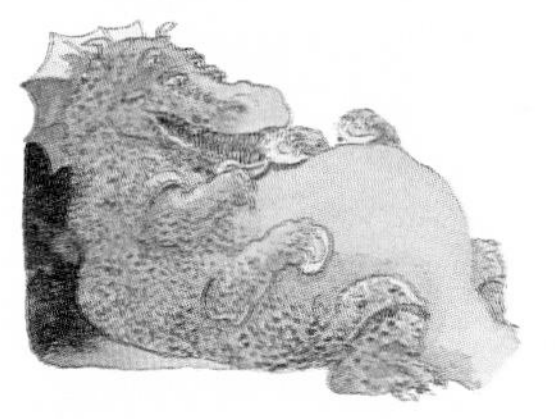

Illustrated by
Michael Foreman

PUFFIN BOOKS

Also by Terry Jones and Michael Foreman in Picture Puffin

A FISH OF THE WORLD

Also in Picture Puffin

DINOSAURS AND ALL THAT RUBBISH *Michael Foreman*
LONG NECK AND THUNDER FOOT *Helen Piers/Michael Foreman*
TEENY TINY AND THE WITCH-WOMAN *Barbara Walker/Michael Foreman*
THE GREAT WHITE MAN-EATING SHARK *Margaret Mahy/Jonathan Allen*
BEWARE OF BOYS *Tony Blundell*
PUSS IN BOOTS *Tony Ross*

PUFFIN BOOKS

Published by the Penguin Group
Penguin Books Ltd, 27 Wrights Lane, London W8 5TZ, England
Penguin Books USA Inc., 375 Hudson Street, New York, New York 10014, USA
Penguin Books Australia Ltd, Ringwood, Victoria, Australia
Penguin Books Canada Ltd, 10 Alcorn Avenue, Toronto, Ontario, Canada M4V 3B2
Penguin Books (NZ) Ltd, 182–190 Wairau Road, Auckland 10, New Zealand

Penguin Books Ltd, Registered Offices: Harmondsworth, Middlesex, England

This story originally appeared in *Fairy Tales* by Terry Jones,
illustrated by Michael Foreman, first published by Pavilion Books Ltd 1981
Published separately by Pavilion Books Ltd 1993
Published in Picture Puffins 1995
10 9 8 7 6 5 4 3 2 1

Designed by Bet Ayer

Made and printed in Italy by Printers srl – Trento

A long time ago, in a land far away, the most terrible beast that ever lived roamed the countryside. It had four eyes, six legs and a thousand teeth. In the morning it would gobble up men as they went to work in the fields. In the afternoon it would break into lonely farms and eat up mothers and children as they sat down to lunch, and at night it would stalk the streets of the towns, looking for its supper.

In the biggest of all the towns, there lived a pastry cook and his wife, and they had a small son whose name was Sam. One morning, as Sam was helping his father to make pastries, he heard that the Mayor had offered a reward of ten bags of gold to anyone who could rid the city of the beast.

'Oh,' said Sam, 'wouldn't I just like to win those ten bags of gold!'

'Nonsense!' said his father. 'Put those pastries in the oven.'

That afternoon they heard that the King himself had offered a reward of a hundred bags of gold to anyone who could rid the kingdom of the beast.

'Oooh! Wouldn't I just like to win those hundred bags of gold,' said Sam.

'You're too small,' said his father. 'Now run along and take those cakes to the palace before it gets dark.'

So Sam set off for the palace with a tray of cakes balanced on his head. But he was so busy thinking of the hundred bags of gold that he lost his way, and soon it began to grow dark.

'Oh dear!' said Sam. 'The beast will be coming soon to look for his supper. I'd better hurry home.'

So he turned and started to hurry home as fast as he could. But he was utterly and completely lost, and he didn't know which way to turn. Soon it grew very dark. The streets were deserted, and everyone was safe inside, and had bolted and barred their doors for fear of the beast.

Poor Sam ran up this street and down the next, but he couldn't find the way home. Then suddenly – in the distance – he heard a sound like thunder, and he knew that the beast with a thousand teeth was approaching the city!

Sam ran up to the nearest house, and started to bang on the door.

'Let me in!' he cried. 'I'm out in the streets, and the beast is approaching the city! Listen!' And he could hear the sound of the beast getting nearer and nearer. The ground shook and the windows rattled in their frames. But the people inside said no – if they opened the door, the beast might get in and eat them too.

So poor Sam ran up to the next house, and banged as hard as he could on their door, but the people told him to go away.

Then he heard a roar, and he heard the beast coming down the street, and he ran as hard as he could. But no matter how hard he ran, he could hear the beast getting nearer . . . and nearer . . . And he glanced over his shoulder – and there it was at the end of the street! Poor Sam in his fright dropped his tray, and hid under some steps. And the beast got nearer and nearer until it was right on top of him, and it bent down and its terrible jaws went SNACK! and it gobbled up the tray of cakes, and then it turned on Sam.

Sam plucked up all his courage and shouted as loud as he could: 'Don't eat me, Beast! Wouldn't you rather have some more cakes?'

The beast stopped and looked at Sam, and then it looked back at the empty tray, and it said:

'Well . . . they *were* very nice cakes . . . I liked the pink ones particularly. But there are no more left, so I'll just have to eat you . . . ' And it reached under the steps where poor Sam was hiding, and pulled him out in its great horny claws.

'Oh . . . p-p-please!' cried Sam. 'If you don't eat me, I'll make you some more. I'll make you lots of good things, for I'm the son of the best pastry cook in the land.'

'Will you make more of those pink ones?' asked the beast.

'Oh yes! I'll make as many pink ones as you can eat!' cried Sam.

'Very well,' said the beast, and put poor Sam in its pocket, and carried him home to its lair.

The beast lived in a dark and dismal cave. The floor was littered with the bones of the people it had eaten, and the stone walls were marked with lines, where the beast used to sharpen its teeth. But Sam got to work

right away, and started to bake as many cakes as he could for the beast. And when he ran out of flour or eggs or anything else, the beast would run back into town to get them, although it never paid for anything.

Sam cooked and baked, and he made scones and éclairs and meringues and sponge cakes and shortbread and doughnuts. But the beast looked at them and said, 'You haven't made any pink ones!'

'Just a minute!' said Sam, and he took all the cakes and he covered every one of them in pink icing.

'There you are,' said Sam, 'they're *all* pink ones!'

'Great!' said the beast and ate the lot.

Well, the beast grew so fond of Sam's cakes that it shortly gave up eating people altogether, and it stayed at home in its cave, eating and eating and growing fatter and fatter. This went on for a whole year, until one morning Sam woke up to find the beast rolling around groaning and beating the floor of the cave. Of course you can guess what was the matter with it.

'Oh dear,' said Sam, 'I'm afraid it's all that pink icing that has given you toothache.'

Well, the toothache got worse and worse and, because the beast had a thousand teeth, it was soon suffering from the worst toothache that anyone in the whole history of the world has ever suffered from. It lay on its side and held its head and roared in agony, until Sam began to feel quite sorry for it. The beast howled and howled with pain, until it could stand it no longer. 'Please, Sam, help me!' it cried.

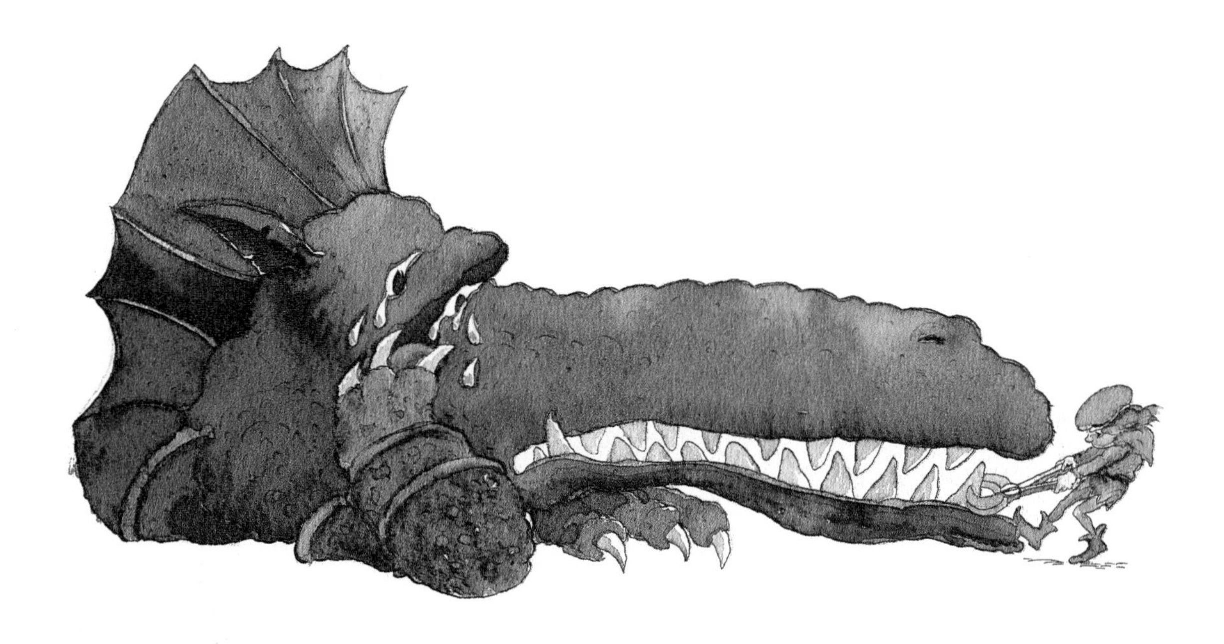

'Very well,' said Sam. 'Sit still and open your mouth.'

So the beast sat very still and opened its mouth while Sam got a pair of pliers and took out every single tooth in that beast's head.

Well, when the beast had lost all its thousand teeth, it couldn't eat people any more. So Sam took it home and went to the Mayor and claimed ten bags of gold as his reward.

Then he went to the King and claimed the hundred bags of gold as his reward. Then he went back and lived with his father and mother once more, and the beast helped in the pastry shop, and took cakes to the palace every day, and everyone forgot they had ever been afraid of the beast with a thousand teeth.